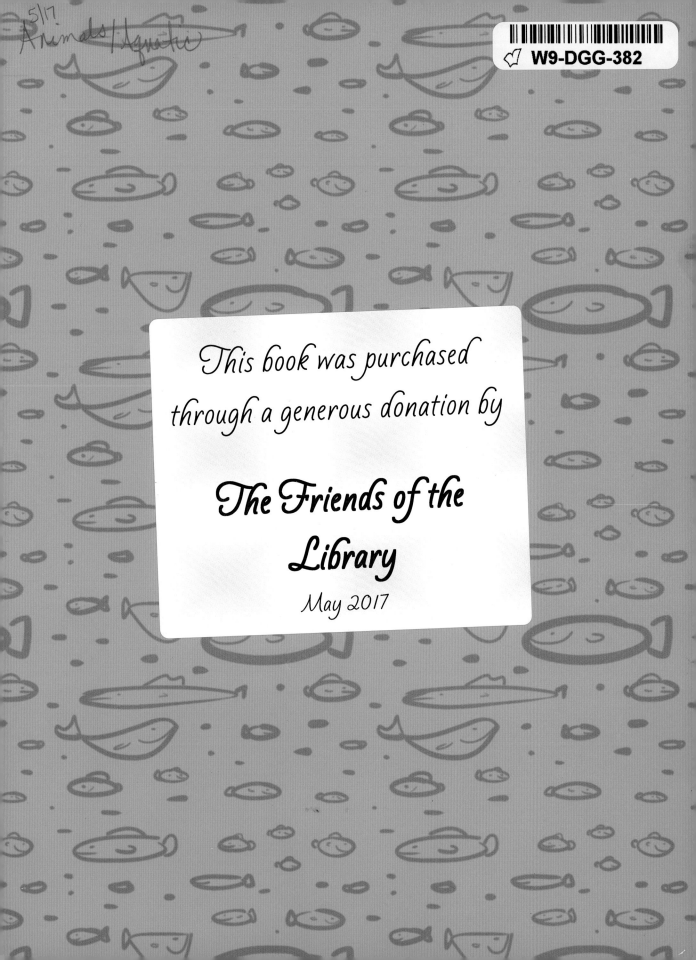

Brittany R. Jacobs

THE KRAKEN'S RULES FOR MAKING FRIENDS

BROOKLYN, NY

Many monsters call the deep sea home,

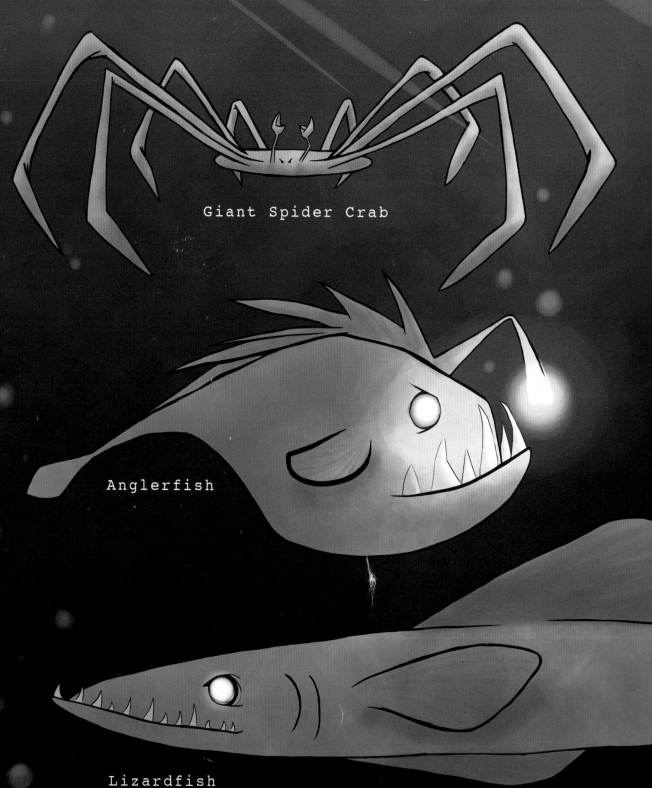

Giant Spider Crab

Anglerfish

Lizardfish

...the
KRAKEN!

Where did everyone go?

Why don't they like me?

Maybe I should
try to be...

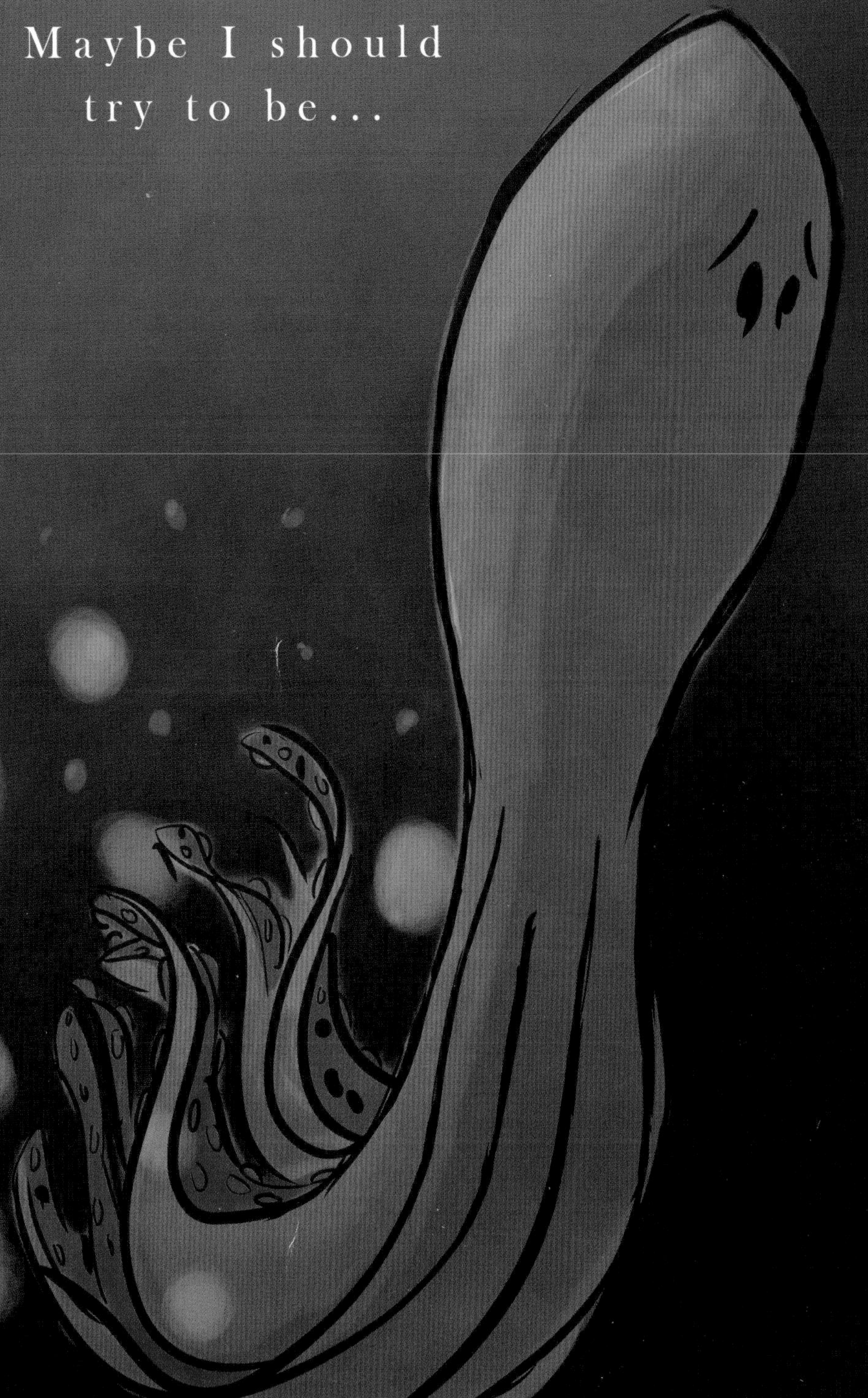

someone else.

"Hey friends! What's crackin'?
I'm Koi!"
lied the Kraken.

"Something smells fishy,"
said the Manta Ray.
"You're awfully big for a Koi."

"That's because he's not a Koi!"
shrieked the Tuna.

"He's the

KRAKEN!!!"

WHY won't ANYONE be my FRIEND?!

What's SO BAD about me?!

I'M REALLY VERY NICE!

Even the Great White Shark has friends.

"How does he do it?"
wondered the Kraken.

Maybe I should ask him.

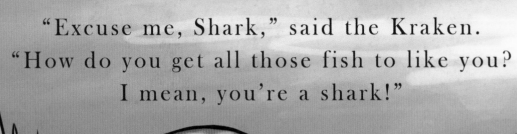

"Excuse me, Shark," said the Kraken.
"How do you get all those fish to like you?
I mean, you're a shark!"

"How does a Kraken make friends?
I'm tired of being all alone."

"There's no reason to have a sea cow,"
replied the Shark.
"Wipe away those tears, because all
you have to do is follow these
Rules for Making Friends."

**"And rule number one is,
KEEP YOUR COOL!**
No one likes a pouting fish."

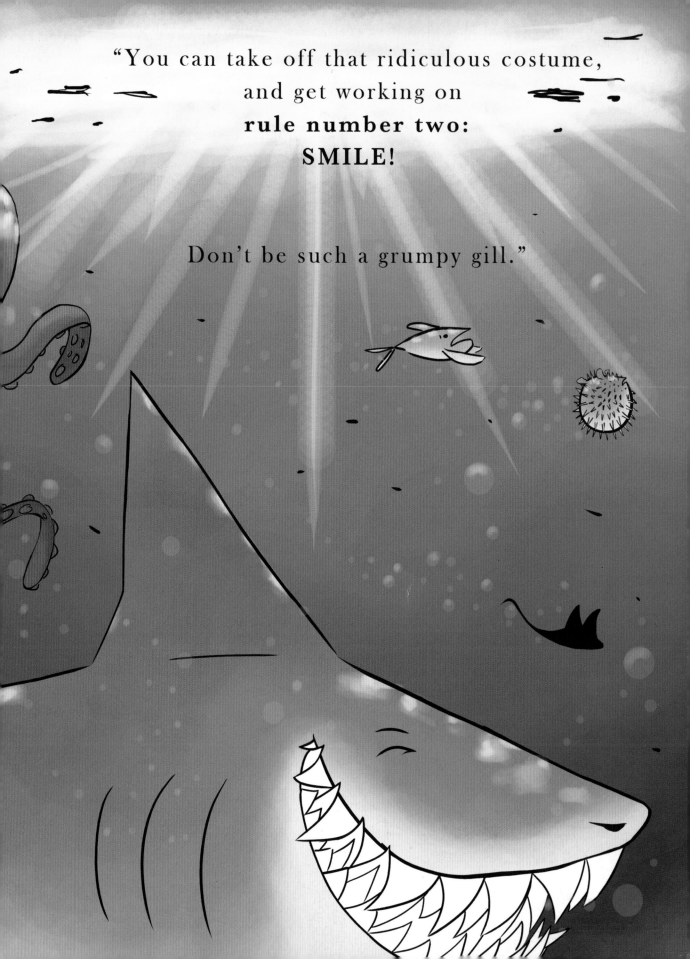

"You can take off that ridiculous costume,
and get working on
rule number two:
SMILE!

Don't be such a grumpy gill."

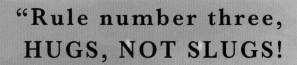

"Rule number three,
HUGS, NOT SLUGS!

You've got to let fish know
you care."

I just want a hug!

"Don't keep all the goods to yourself!"

"**Rule number five,**" said the Shark.
"**LEND A HELPING FIN,**
or tentacle in your case."

"**Rule number six** for making friends: **BE YOURSELF!**"

"But I'm the Kraken."

"And I'm a Great White Shark."

"Some things cannot be helped, so you have got to make the best of what you've got. Go get 'em!"

With that, the Kraken floated over to the group and...

They all screamed and swam away.

Well, all but one.

For my biggest fan, G. Cindy,
& my main squeeze, BT

Published in the United States by POW!
a division of powerHouse Packaging & Supply, Inc.
37 Main Street, Brooklyn, NY 11201-1021
telephone 718-801-8376
email info@POWkidsbooks.com

www.POWkidsbooks.com
www.powerHouseBooks.com
www.powerHousePackaging.com

Library of Congress Control Number: 2016936609

ISBN 978-1-57687-814-9

10 9 8 7 6 5 4 3 2 1

Printed in Malaysia